Clarice Bean

That's Me

Lauren Child

This story is for Pat.
We met when I was
seven and she has
been feeding me
chocolate brownies
ever since.
She is also a very
good friend.

PAT

LAUREN

a special thank you
to Emily who is
of course
the bee's knees

minal is a
bug

eggs
milk
bread
celery
chocolate
thank you
to the chic
caroline
valentine

ORCHARD BOOKS
First published in Great Britain in 1999
by Orchard Books
This edition published in 2014
by The Watts Publishing Group
10 9 8 7 6
Copyright © Lauren Child, 1999 and 2009

The moral rights
of the author and
illustrator have
been asserted.
All rights reserved.
A CIP catalogue record
for this book is available
from the British Library.

ISBN 978 1 40830 004 6
Printed and bound
in China.
Orchard Books
An imprint of Hachette
Children's Group. Part of
The Watts Publishing Group
Carmelite House
50 Victoria Embankment
London EC4Y 0DZ.

An Hachette UK Company
www.hachette.co.uk
www.hachettechildrens.co.uk

This is me
Clarice Bean

(I haven't got
a watch so I've drawn
one on my arm in biro.)

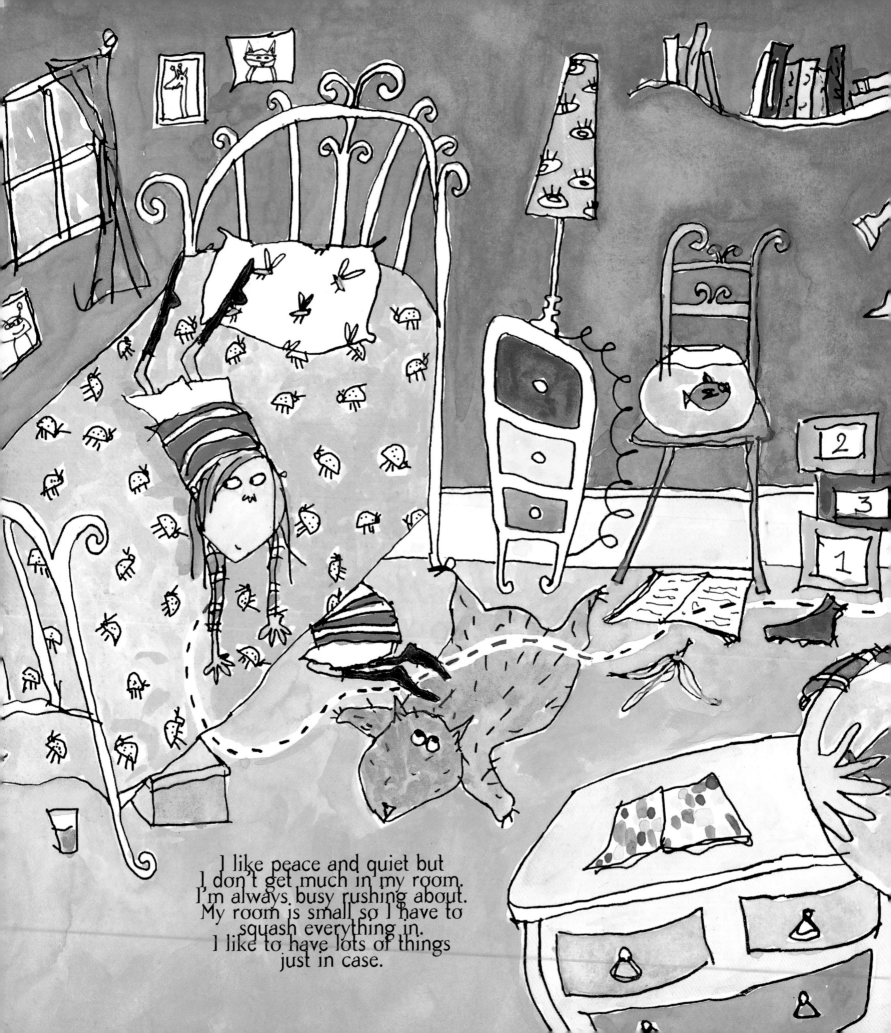

I like peace and quiet but
I don't get much in my room.
I'm always busy rushing about.
My room is small so I have to
squash everything in.
I like to have lots of things
just in case.

I have this
younger brother
Minal Cricket.

We have to share so I have drawn a line down the middle.

If he puts one toe
over my side
he is sorry.

Sometimes I say,
I haven't got time for
all your nonsense.

Minal Cricket likes to hang upside down until he turns purple.
Then he sort of wriggles around like a maggot.

And he says, Twit.

And I say,
Twit and a half.

And he says,
Twit with carrots
in your ears.

And then I flick his nose with my ruler.

And he says,
Muuum,

in this really whiney brother way.

And Mum says,
No flicking noses
with rulers.

And I say,
What do you flick
noses with then?

And she says,
Celery.

And I say,
We've run out.

And she says,
No flicking noses then.

My sister Marcie has a room of her own,
so she has peace and quiet whenever she fancies.
Marcie likes to wear make-up and read about boys.
When I have time on my hands I peep
round the door and try to make her
notice me.

She says,
Go away.
And I say,
Why?
**Because
I don't want to talk to you.**
Why?
**Because
you are very irritating.**
Why?
**Because
you are a little brat.**
Why?
**You better get
out of my room
before I count to ten.**

And I don't need to ask why.

Maarcie

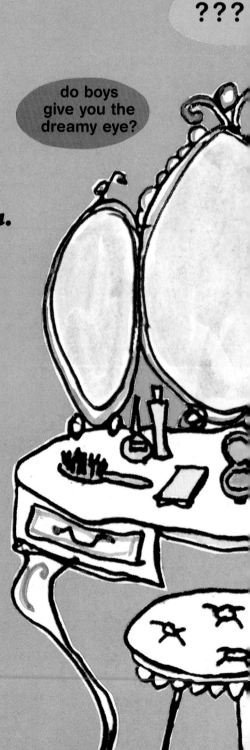

???

do boys
give you the
dreamy eye?

My
older
brother
Kurt is usually
in his room with
his door shut.
He doesn't talk much
but he wears T-shirts
with writing on them.
They say,

SHUT UP AND GO AWAY.

Mum says,
He's at that difficult age.
Dad says,
He should try being
forty-four.
Mum says,
*It's not easy
being a teenager.*

Dad says,
It's no **picnic** being the father of one and it would **help** if he would stop grunting.

no entry nuclear waste

Mum says,
He's in the dark tunnel of adolescence.
But usually he's in his room.

Kurt says,
No one understands me.

happy about nothing

Shut up
Go away

bored beyond belief

Kurt says he wants to be left alone. Lucky for him he has a room all to himself and it smells of socks.

I'm going **bananas** here Bernard.

It's all right for Dad.
When he wants to be
left alone he goes to work.

He has a smart marbly office.
It's wall to wall windows
and office equipment.
He has a swivelling chair
and a desk the size of a bed.
It's full of important business
and you can only get to talk
to him if Ms Egglington
buzzes you through.
When Dad wants some peace
and quiet Ms Egglington says,

I'm afraid he's in a meeting.

(i.e. buzz off.)
Really he's eating tutti-frutti
ice cream and listening to
Frank Sinatra on the stereo.

I can't talk now,
I've got another
call coming through.

This thing's going
down faster than
a sinking soufflé.

you're dum dee dum dee dum Waldorf Salad

Grandad spends all his time having peace and quiet.
He is most often asleep in a chair with a cat on his head.

My brother Minal and I
like to jump on him and snip his
moustache with Mum's nail scissors.

Sometimes Grandad and me play snap.
Grandad's eyesight is on the blink
so normally I win.
He says,
Is that a Jack of Hearts?
And I say, No, it's a
Three of Spades,
Grandad.

Yesterday he poured a carton
of soup on his cornflakes.
He said,
I think this milk's off.
It looks a bit lumpy.
I said, It's pea soup, Grandad.

When Mum wants some peace and quiet she balances on one leg in her bedroom or listens to whales singing in the bath.

Sometimes she has candles round the edge that smell. Other times she plays one of her "learn a foreign language in a fortnight" tapes.

She's doing Mandarin at the moment.
So far she can say, I've spilt custard on my cardigan,
and there's a spider hiding in my hotel room.

She likes speaking in other languages.
It makes her feel like she is on holiday.
Sometimes she'll say, Jeg er dødtræt af jer allesammen, which means "I've had it up to here with the lot of you" in Danish.

Sometimes I say,
Mum do you ever get bored
and she says, The chance would be a fine thing.

When I get a bee in my bonnet and Mum needs some
peace and quiet she says,

Go and run about in the garden.

This usually does the trick.

Sometimes I chuck potatoes
over next door's wall.

Because I might want to be an acrobat I have to keep nimble and flexible. I do this by scrinching into the laundry basket.

Getting out is the tricky bit.

I do **balancing** and smiling in tights.

(That's a very important part of acrobatics.)

There's no peace and quiet in the garden
because there's this boy who lives next door.
He likes to call over the wall.
He says,

What are you **doing?**
Can I-I-I **play?**
I knooow you can **hear me.**

Grandad calls him Shouting Boy, but I call him Robert Granger.
He always wants to know what I'm up to, and he always wants
to do what I'm doing, which is normally twirling until I fall over.

Robert Granger doesn't have any ideas of his own
except copying me.

So I go indoors to do handstands quietly on my side of the room.

Then Minal starts playing football on my bed. He says he does it "accidentally".

I say,

More like accidentally on purpose.

I get cross. So I "accidentally" chuck his duvet out of the window. It lands on next door's dog and Dad gets in a row with the neighbours.

Dad says,
Right now you are
not the flavour of
the month,
young lady.
Minal is grinning
like a pleased twit
so I tip a bowl of
spaghetti hoops
on his head.

I am in

big

trouble.

Mum says I should try to think before I act.
And she's right.
If I'd thought about it I would have put
  rhubarb crumble down his trousers.

I am in such big trouble that I get sent to my room for 3 whole hours.

I love it.

It's the best piece of peace and quiet I've had in ages.

The only time my family is quiet at the same time is when we sit down to watch our favourite show – Martians in the Kitchen.

The rest of the time it is non-stop noise but that's the way we like it.

uncle Ted
(eating again)

Marcie
(painting
her toes)

kurt
(smiling)

Yolla

Dad

Mum

Noah

minal Cricket
(not talking)

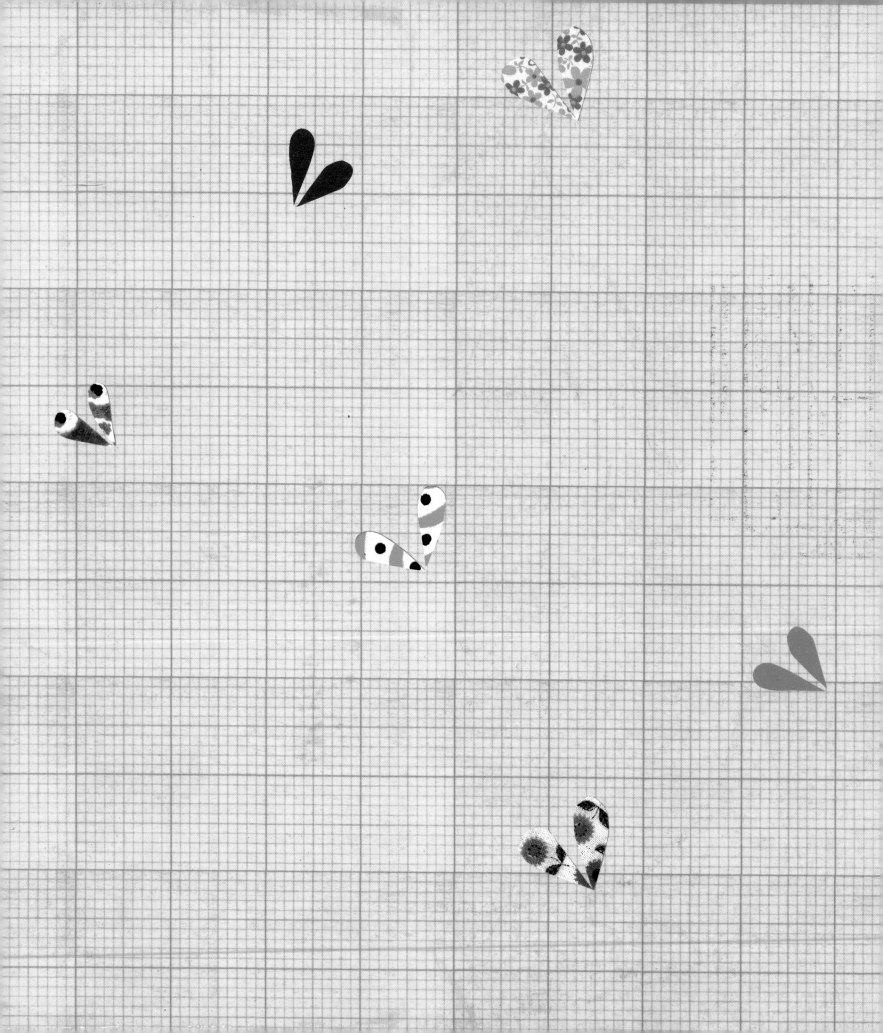